For Bess

First published 1998 by Walker Books Ltd
87 Vauxhall Walk, London SE11 5HJ

10 9 8 7 6 5 4 3 2 1

© 1998 Kim Lewis

This book has been typeset in Sabon.

Printed in Italy

British Library Cataloguing in Publication Data
A catalogue record for this book is
available from the British Library.

ISBN 0-7445-6129-9

Just
like
Floss

KIM LEWIS

WALKER BOOKS
AND SUBSIDIARIES
LONDON • BOSTON • SYDNEY

One night in winter
Floss lay in the hay
with her newborn
collie puppies.
She licked them dry
and kept them warm
as snow fell
against the barn.

"Dad, can we
keep a puppy?"
the children asked.
"Maybe," their father
said. "We could use
another collie just like
Floss to work with
the sheep on the farm."

The children watched
the puppies grow and gave
each one a name.

"Dad, we love them all," they said.
"Which one would be the best?"
"Wait and see,"
their father said.

Bess and Nell played tug-of-war.

Cap and Jack played hide-and-seek.

The littlest, Sam, kept following Floss.

She licked his ears and nose and barked.

"What does Floss tell Sam?"

the children asked.

Floss went back
to work with Dad,
gathering sheep
on the farm.
"Come on, pups!"
the children said
and took them all
outside. Bess and Nell
played tug-of-war.
Cap and Jack played
hide-and-seek.
Sam went looking
for his mother.

Sam ran in the snow.
He jumped in the drifts
by a hole in the fence.
He chased after snowflakes
into the field. Sheep looked up
at the sight of a puppy.
Curious, they came closer.

Sheep gathered around and stared at Sam. Their breath blew hot in the cold snowy air. Sam looked at the big woolly shapes with their hard black heads and horns.

One ewe put her head down
to sniff at Sam. She was big
and Sam was little. Sam wanted
to run but he stayed very still.
He looked in the old ewe's eyes.

Slowly the ewe began
backing away.
Sam crouched low
and started to run.
With a clicking of heels,
all the sheep scattered.
"Sam!" cried the children.
"Sam, come here!"

Sam tripped in the snow
and tumbled over.
The children caught the snowy puppy.
"Big brave Sam!" they said and carried
him back to the barn with Cap
and Jack, Bess and Nell.

Floss was waiting at the barn
with Dad. She licked Sam's
cold wet ears and nose.
"Sam's not afraid of sheep!"
said the children.
"He'll be just like Floss."
"Then we'll keep Sam,"
said Dad, "and find
good homes for all
the others."

The children hugged
the little puppy.
"And we'll love you, Sam,"
they said,
"just like Floss."